D1384977

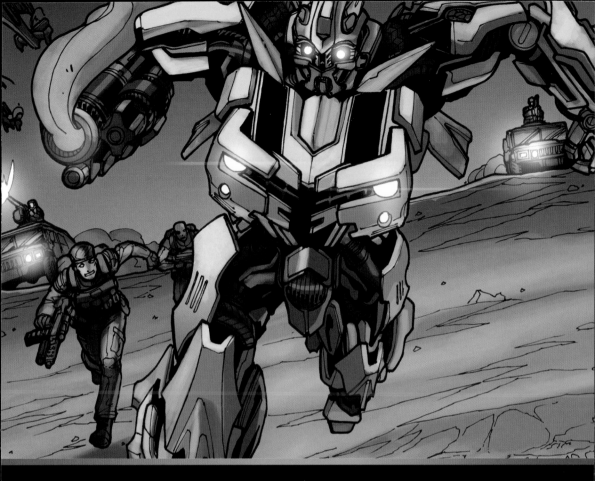

TRANSFORMERS: ALLIANCE

ISSUE NUMBER TWO (OF FOUR)

WRITTEN BY: **CHRIS MOWRY**
ART BY: **ALEX MILNE**
COLORS BY: **JOSH PEREZ**
LETTERS BY: **NEIL UYETAKE**
EDITS BY: **DENTON J. TIPTON**

With the battle of Mission City in the past, the AUTOBOTS prepare to assist their human allies with the removal of the fallen DECEPTICON soldiers. Before they can begin their mission, OPTIMUS PRIME will have to make a difficult decision. Also, somewhere in space, the DECEPTICON warrior known as STARSCREAM, has prepared for perhaps his final battle. Little does he know, however, that things are about to go very wrong.

Special thanks to Hasbro's Aaron Archer, Michael Kelly, Amie Lozanski, Val Roca, Ed Lane, Michael Provost, Erin Hillman, Samantha Lomow, and Michael Verrecchia for their invaluable assistance.

To discuss this issue of ***Transformers***, join the IDW Insiders, or to check out exclusive Web offers, check out our site:

Spotlight

IDW

Licensed by: Hasbro

DreamWorks Pictures

Paramount

GM Official Licensed Product

www.IDWPUBLISHING.com

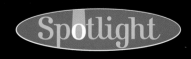

VISIT US AT
www.abdopublishing.com

Reinforced library bound edition published in 2010 by Spotlight, a division of the ABDO Group, 8000 West 78th Street, Edina, Minnesota 55439. Published by agreement with IDW Publishing. www.idwpublishing.com

Printed in the United States of America, Melrose Park, Illinois.
102009
012010

 PRINTED ON RECYCLED PAPER

Library of Congress Cataloging-in-Publication Data

Mowry, Chris.
 Alliance / written by Chris Mowry ; art by Alex Milne ; colors by Josh Perez & Kris Carter ; letters by Chris Mowry & Neil Uyetake.
     v. cm.
 "Transformers, revenge of the fallen, official movie prequel."
 ISBN 978-1-59961-717-6 (vol. 1) -- ISBN 978-1-59961-718-3 (vol. 2)
 ISBN 978-1-59961-719-0 (vol. 3) -- ISBN 978-1-59961-720-6 (vol. 4)
 1. Graphic novels. I. Milne, Alex. II. Transformers, revenge of the fallen (Motion picture) III. Title.
 PZ7.7.M69Al 2010
 741.5'973--dc22
                              2009036393

All Spotlight books have reinforced library bindings and
are manufactured in the United States of America.

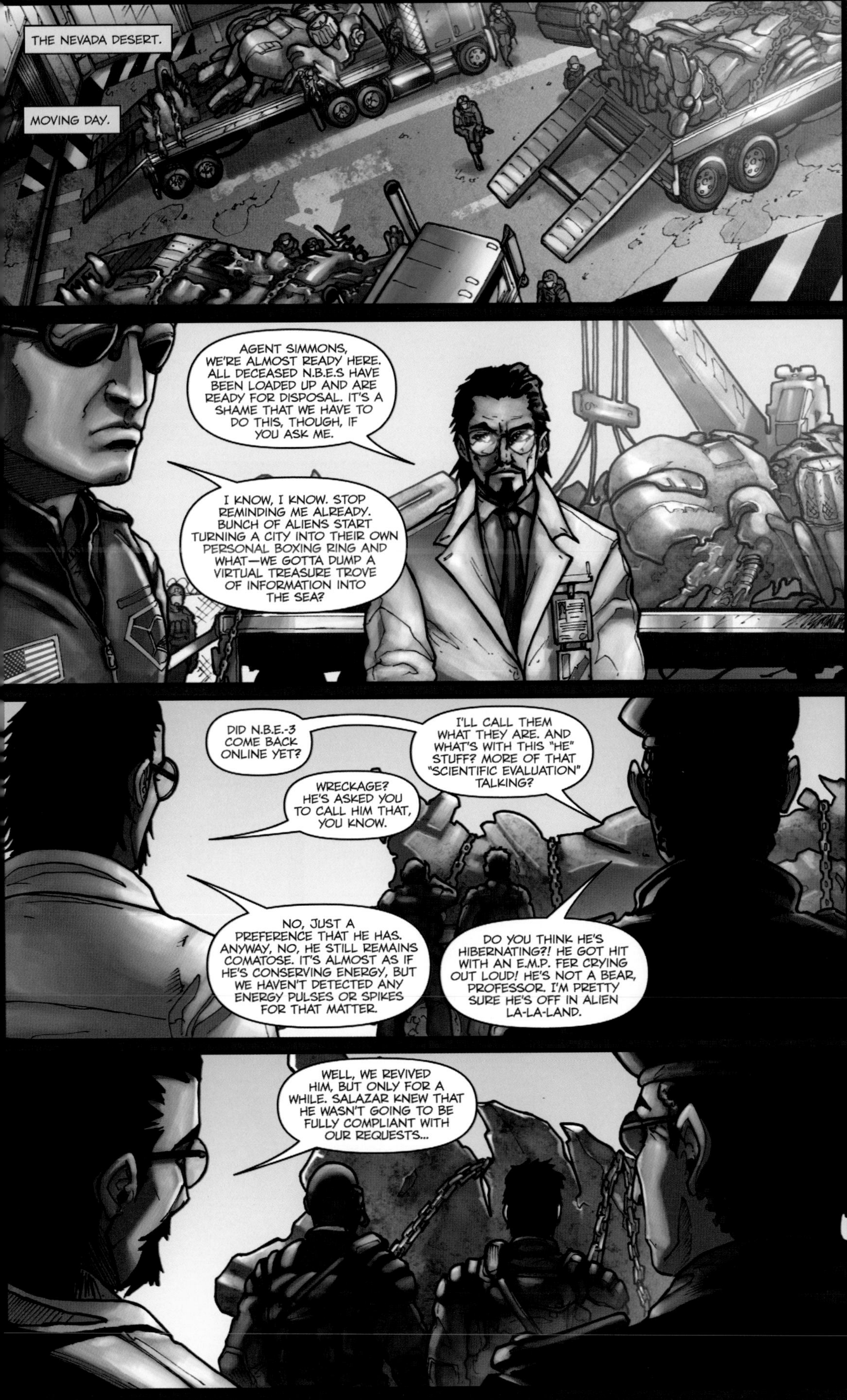
THE NEVADA DESERT.
MOVING DAY.
AGENT SIMMONS, WE'RE ALMOST READY HERE. ALL DECEASED N.B.E.S HAVE BEEN LOADED UP AND ARE READY FOR DISPOSAL. IT'S A SHAME THAT WE HAVE TO DO THIS, THOUGH, IF YOU ASK ME.
I KNOW, I KNOW. STOP REMINDING ME ALREADY. BUNCH OF ALIENS START TURNING A CITY INTO THEIR OWN PERSONAL BOXING RING AND WHAT—WE GOTTA DUMP A VIRTUAL TREASURE TROVE OF INFORMATION INTO THE SEA?
DID N.B.E.-3 COME BACK ONLINE YET?
WRECKAGE? HE'S ASKED YOU TO CALL HIM THAT, YOU KNOW.
I'LL CALL THEM WHAT THEY ARE. AND WHAT'S WITH THIS "HE" STUFF? MORE OF THAT "SCIENTIFIC EVALUATION" TALKING?
NO, JUST A PREFERENCE THAT HE HAS. ANYWAY, NO, HE STILL REMAINS COMATOSE. IT'S ALMOST AS IF HE'S CONSERVING ENERGY, BUT WE HAVEN'T DETECTED ANY ENERGY PULSES OR SPIKES FOR THAT MATTER.
DO YOU THINK HE'S HIBERNATING?! HE GOT HIT WITH AN E.M.P. FER CRYING OUT LOUD! HE'S NOT A BEAR, PROFESSOR. I'M PRETTY SURE HE'S OFF IN ALIEN LA-LA-LAND.
WELL, WE REVIVED HIM, BUT ONLY FOR A WHILE. SALAZAR KNEW THAT HE WASN'T GOING TO BE FULLY COMPLIANT WITH OUR REQUESTS...

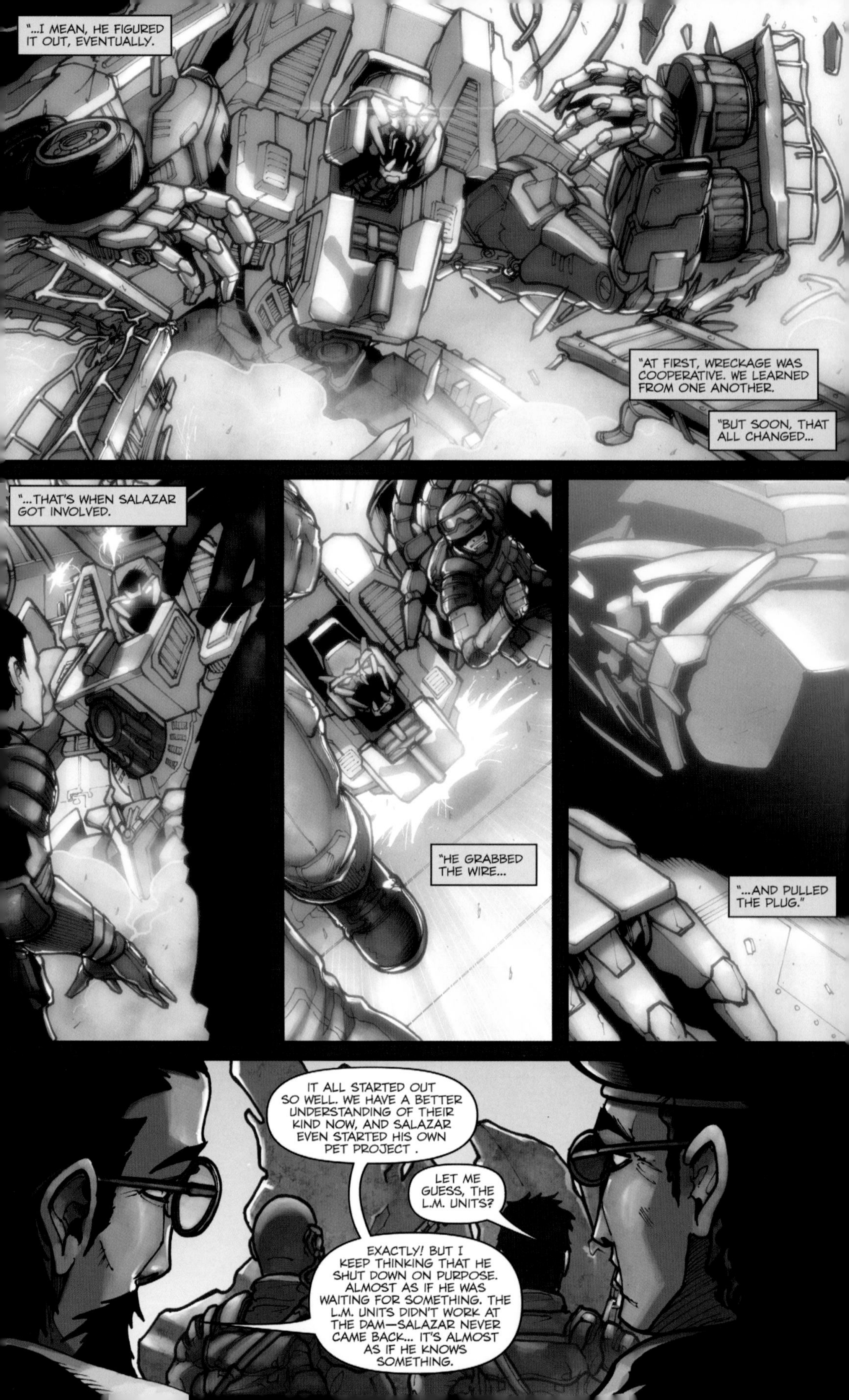
"...I MEAN, HE FIGURED IT OUT, EVENTUALLY.
"AT FIRST, WRECKAGE WAS COOPERATIVE. WE LEARNED FROM ONE ANOTHER.
"BUT SOON, THAT ALL CHANGED...
"...THAT'S WHEN SALAZAR GOT INVOLVED.
"HE GRABBED THE WIRE...
"...AND PULLED THE PLUG."
IT ALL STARTED OUT SO WELL. WE HAVE A BETTER UNDERSTANDING OF THEIR KIND NOW, AND SALAZAR EVEN STARTED HIS OWN PET PROJECT .
LET ME GUESS, THE L.M. UNITS?
EXACTLY! BUT I KEEP THINKING THAT HE SHUT DOWN ON PURPOSE. ALMOST AS IF HE WAS WAITING FOR SOMETHING. THE L.M. UNITS DIDN'T WORK AT THE DAM—SALAZAR NEVER CAME BACK... IT'S ALMOST AS IF HE KNOWS SOMETHING.

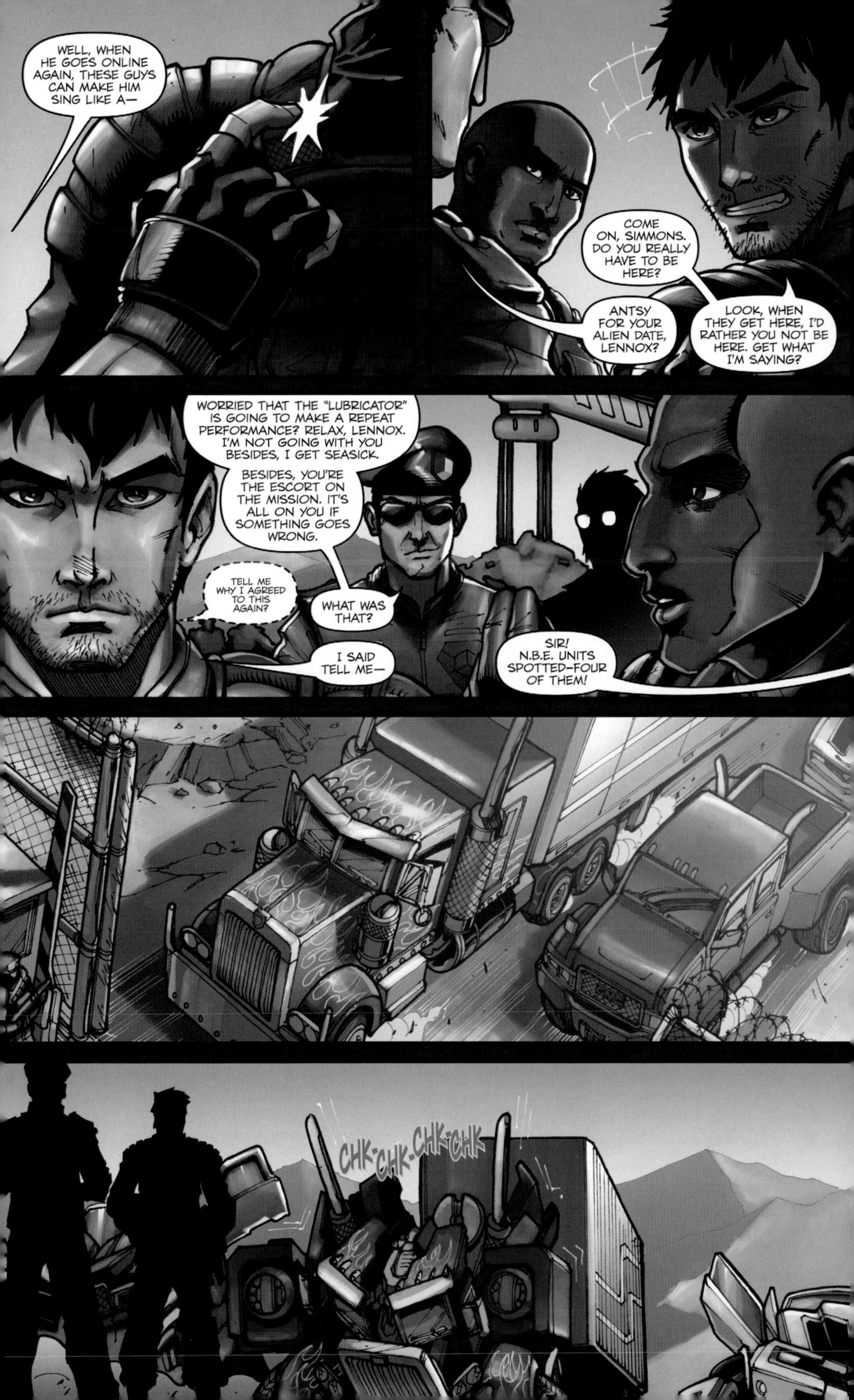

WELL, WHEN HE GOES ONLINE AGAIN, THESE GUYS CAN MAKE HIM SING LIKE A—
COME ON, SIMMONS. DO YOU REALLY HAVE TO BE HERE?
ANTSY FOR YOUR ALIEN DATE, LENNOX?
LOOK, WHEN THEY GET HERE, I'D RATHER YOU NOT BE HERE. GET WHAT I'M SAYING?
WORRIED THAT THE "LUBRICATOR" IS GOING TO MAKE A REPEAT PERFORMANCE? RELAX, LENNOX. I'M NOT GOING WITH YOU BESIDES, I GET SEASICK.
BESIDES, YOU'RE THE ESCORT ON THE MISSION. IT'S ALL ON YOU IF SOMETHING GOES WRONG.
TELL ME WHY I AGREED TO THIS AGAIN?
WHAT WAS THAT?
I SAID TELL ME—
SIR! N.B.E. UNITS SPOTTED—FOUR OF THEM!
CHK-CHK-CHK-CHK

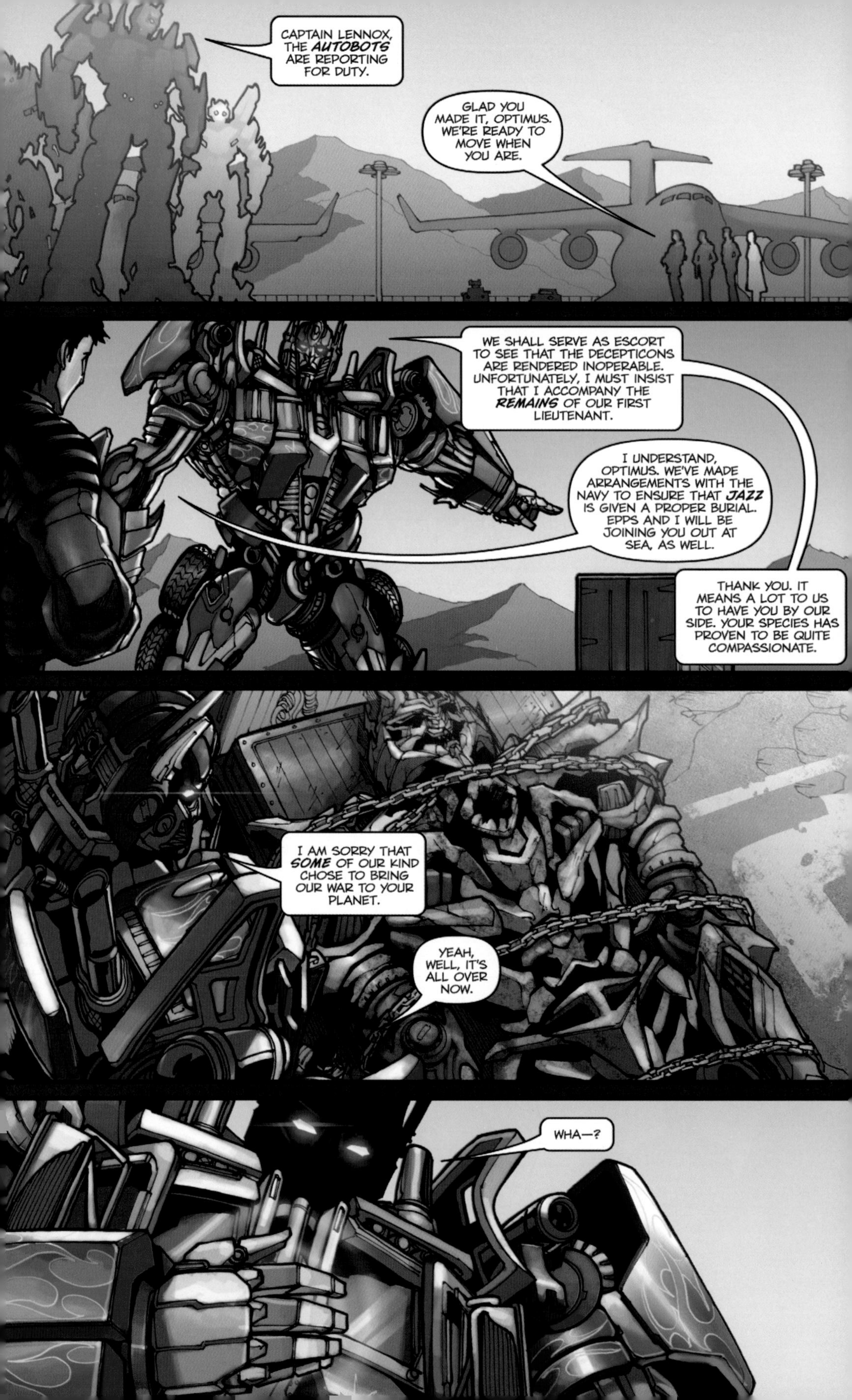
CAPTAIN LENNOX, THE AUTOBOTS ARE REPORTING FOR DUTY.
GLAD YOU MADE IT, OPTIMUS. WE'RE READY TO MOVE WHEN YOU ARE.
WE SHALL SERVE AS ESCORT TO SEE THAT THE DECEPTICONS ARE RENDERED INOPERABLE. UNFORTUNATELY, I MUST INSIST THAT I ACCOMPANY THE REMAINS OF OUR FIRST LIEUTENANT.
I UNDERSTAND, OPTIMUS. WE'VE MADE ARRANGEMENTS WITH THE NAVY TO ENSURE THAT JAZZ IS GIVEN A PROPER BURIAL. EPPS AND I WILL BE JOINING YOU OUT AT SEA, AS WELL.
THANK YOU. IT MEANS A LOT TO US TO HAVE YOU BY OUR SIDE. YOUR SPECIES HAS PROVEN TO BE QUITE COMPASSIONATE.
I AM SORRY THAT SOME OF OUR KIND CHOSE TO BRING OUR WAR TO YOUR PLANET.
YEAH, WELL, IT'S ALL OVER NOW.
WHA—?

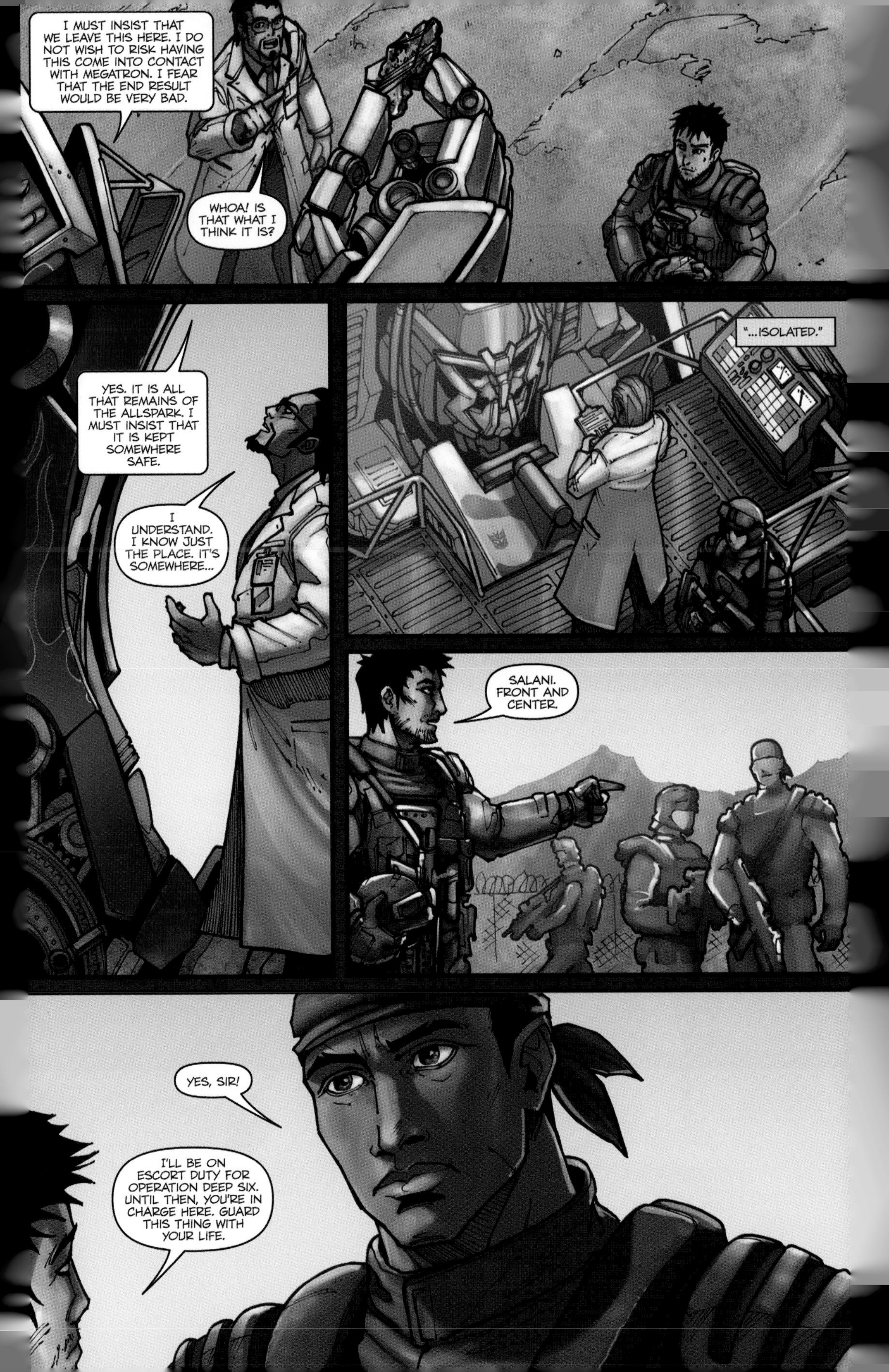
I MUST INSIST THAT WE LEAVE THIS HERE. I DO NOT WISH TO RISK HAVING THIS COME INTO CONTACT WITH MEGATRON. I FEAR THAT THE END RESULT WOULD BE VERY BAD.
WHOA! IS THAT WHAT I THINK IT IS?
YES. IT IS ALL THAT REMAINS OF THE ALLSPARK. I MUST INSIST THAT IT IS KEPT SOMEWHERE SAFE.
I UNDERSTAND. I KNOW JUST THE PLACE. IT'S SOMEWHERE...
"...ISOLATED."
SALANI. FRONT AND CENTER.
YES, SIR!
I'LL BE ON ESCORT DUTY FOR OPERATION DEEP SIX. UNTIL THEN, YOU'RE IN CHARGE HERE. GUARD THIS THING WITH YOUR LIFE.

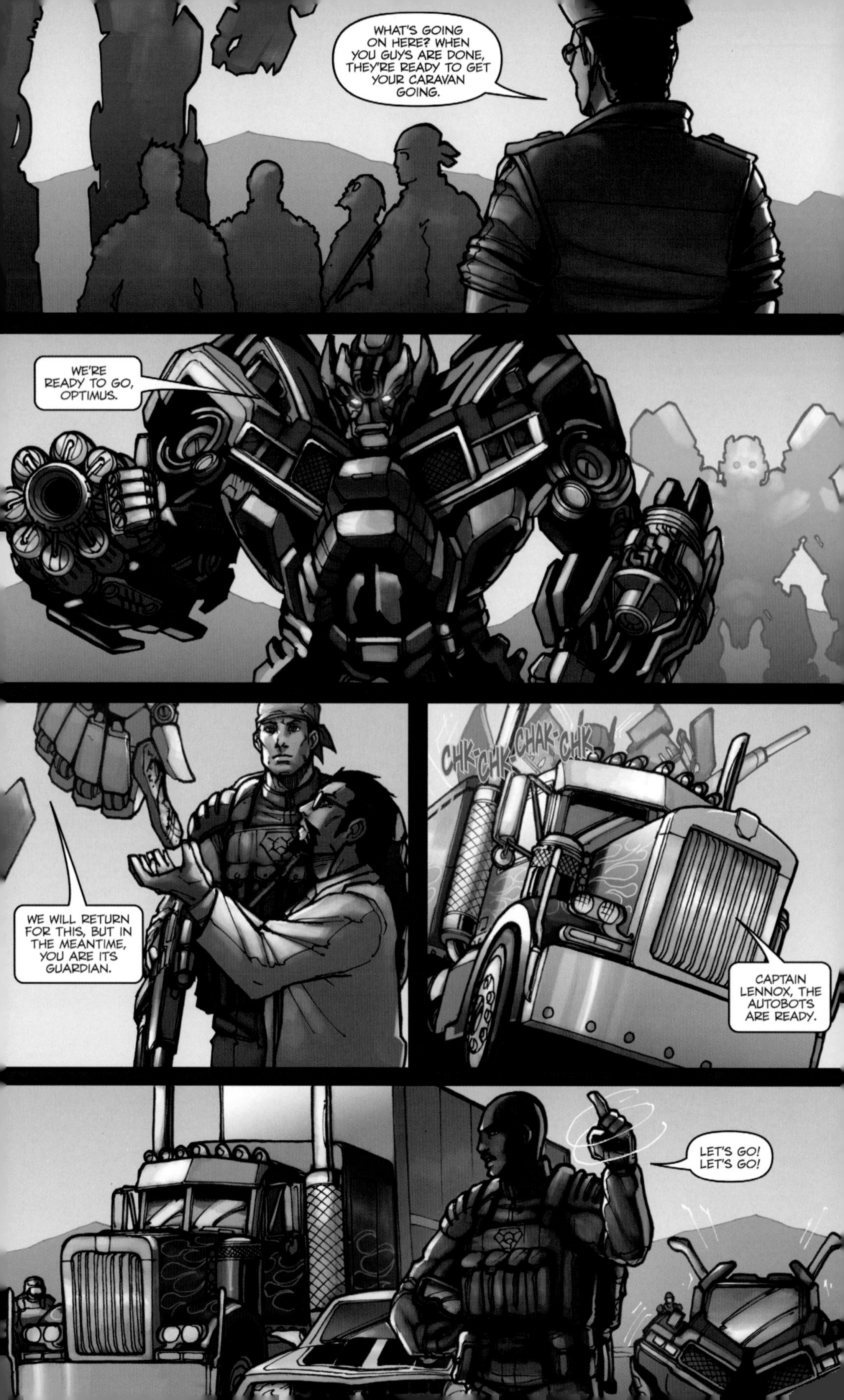
WHAT'S GOING ON HERE? WHEN YOU GUYS ARE DONE, THEY'RE READY TO GET YOUR CARAVAN GOING.
WE'RE READY TO GO, OPTIMUS.
WE WILL RETURN FOR THIS, BUT IN THE MEANTIME, YOU ARE ITS GUARDIAN.
CHK-CHK-CHAK-CHK
CAPTAIN LENNOX, THE AUTOBOTS ARE READY.
LET'S GO! LET'S GO!

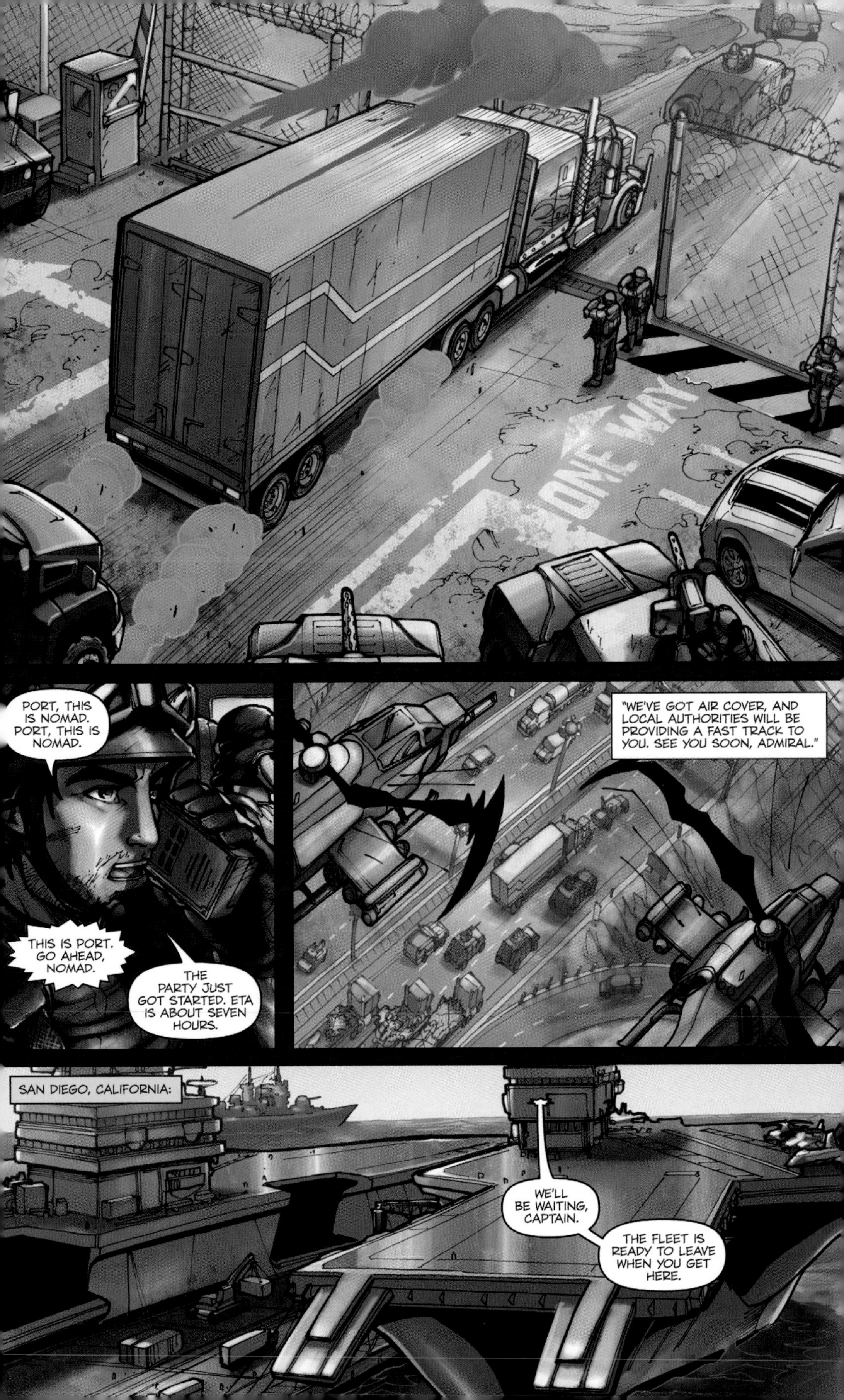

PORT, THIS IS NOMAD. PORT, THIS IS NOMAD.
THIS IS PORT. GO AHEAD, NOMAD.
THE PARTY JUST GOT STARTED. ETA IS ABOUT SEVEN HOURS.
"WE'VE GOT AIR COVER, AND LOCAL AUTHORITIES WILL BE PROVIDING A FAST TRACK TO YOU. SEE YOU SOON, ADMIRAL."
SAN DIEGO, CALIFORNIA:
WE'LL BE WAITING, CAPTAIN.
THE FLEET IS READY TO LEAVE WHEN YOU GET HERE.
ONE WAY

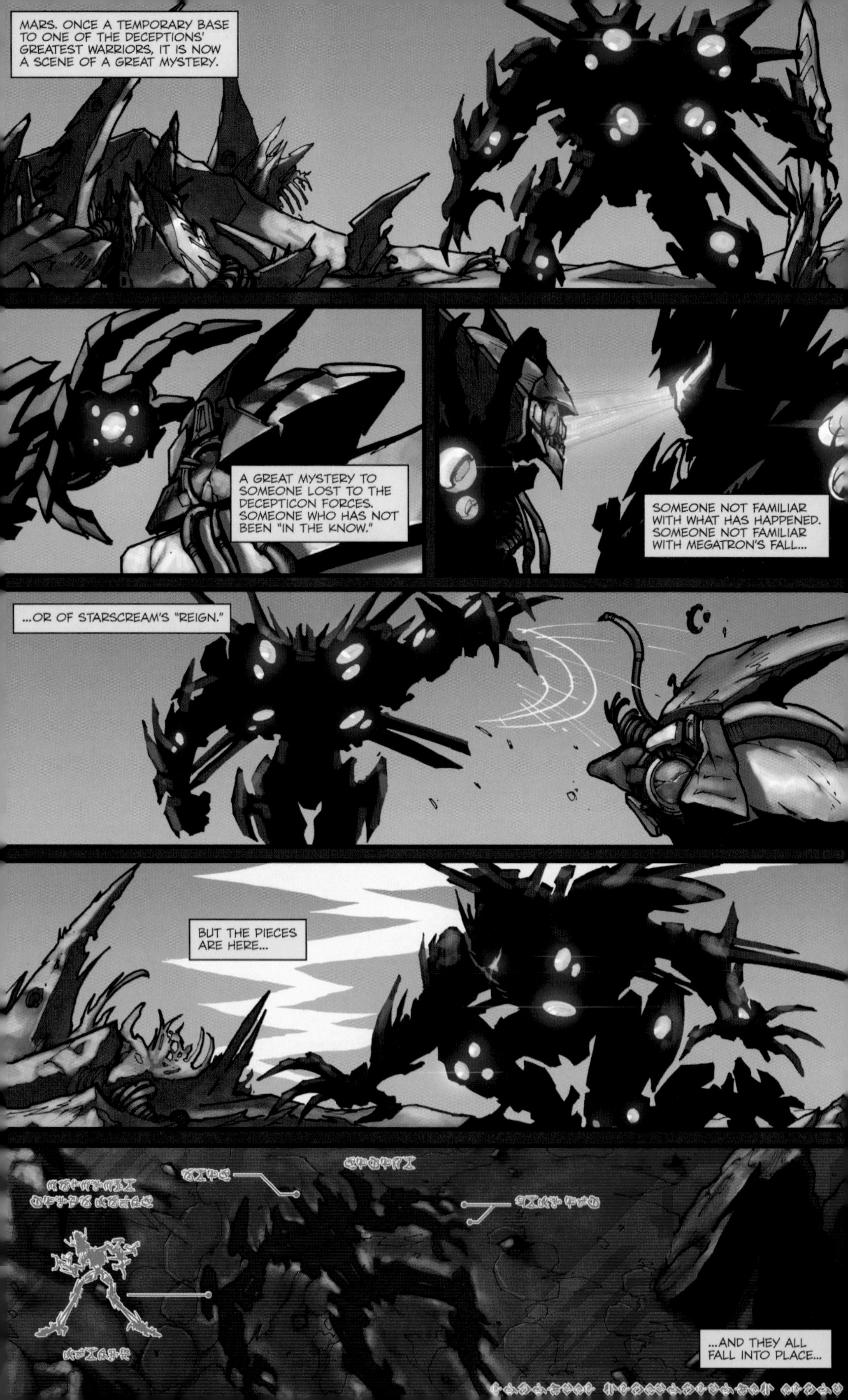
MARS. ONCE A TEMPORARY BASE TO ONE OF THE DECEPTIONS' GREATEST WARRIORS, IT IS NOW A SCENE OF A GREAT MYSTERY.
A GREAT MYSTERY TO SOMEONE LOST TO THE DECEPTICON FORCES. SOMEONE WHO HAS NOT BEEN "IN THE KNOW."
SOMEONE NOT FAMILIAR WITH WHAT HAS HAPPENED. SOMEONE NOT FAMILIAR WITH MEGATRON'S FALL...
...OR OF STARSCREAM'S "REIGN."
BUT THE PIECES ARE HERE...
...AND THEY ALL FALL INTO PLACE...

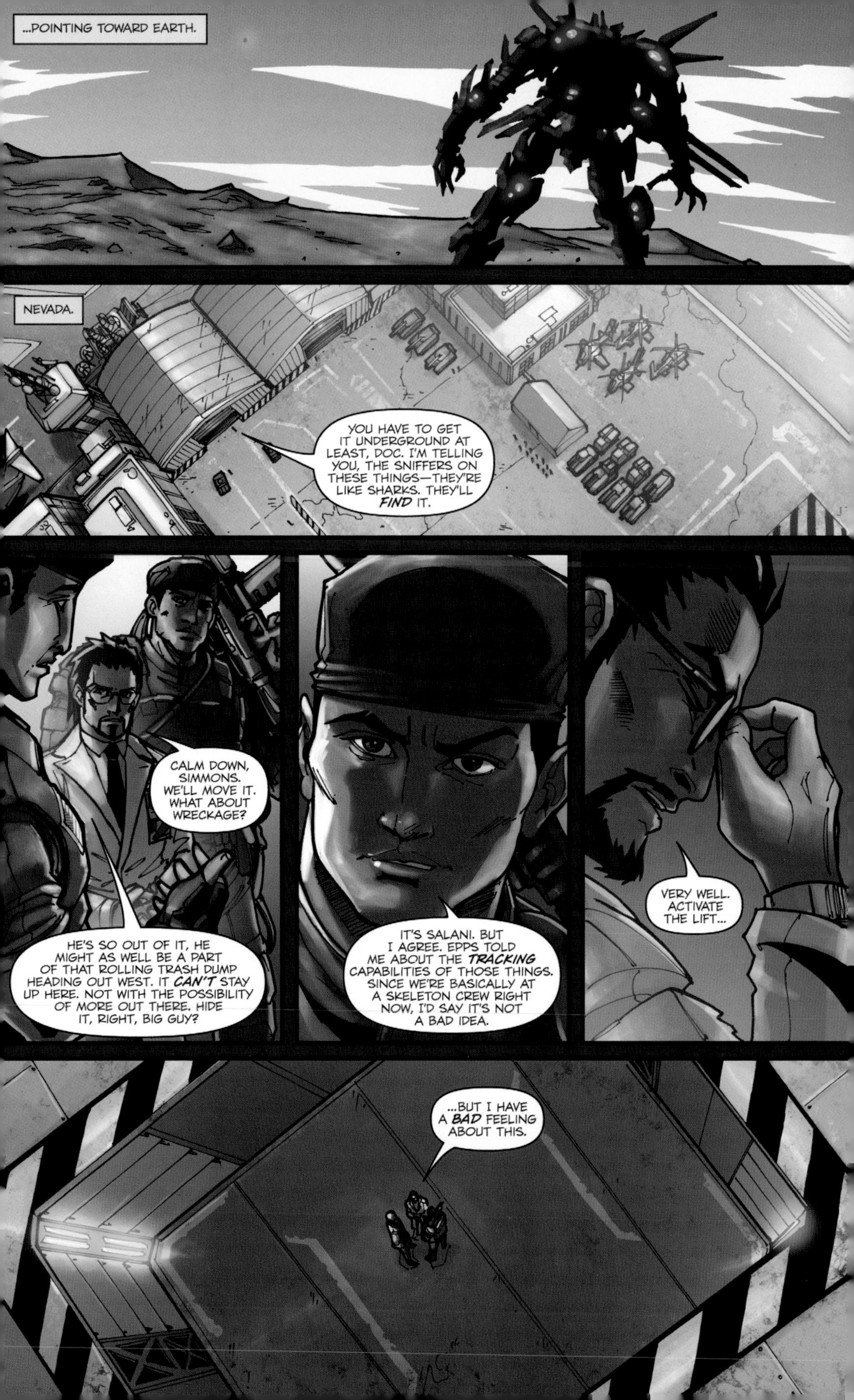
...POINTING TOWARD EARTH.
NEVADA.
YOU HAVE TO GET IT UNDERGROUND AT LEAST, DOC. I'M TELLING YOU, THE SNIFFERS ON THESE THINGS—THEY'RE LIKE SHARKS. THEY'LL *FIND* IT.
CALM DOWN, SIMMONS. WE'LL MOVE IT. WHAT ABOUT WRECKAGE?
HE'S SO OUT OF IT, HE MIGHT AS WELL BE A PART OF THAT ROLLING TRASH DUMP HEADING OUT WEST. IT *CAN'T* STAY UP HERE. NOT WITH THE POSSIBILITY OF MORE OUT THERE. HIDE IT, RIGHT, BIG GUY?
IT'S SALANI. BUT I AGREE. EPPS TOLD ME ABOUT THE *TRACKING* CAPABILITIES OF THOSE THINGS. SINCE WE'RE BASICALLY AT A SKELETON CREW RIGHT NOW, I'D SAY IT'S NOT A BAD IDEA.
VERY WELL. ACTIVATE THE LIFT...
...BUT I HAVE A *BAD* FEELING ABOUT THIS.

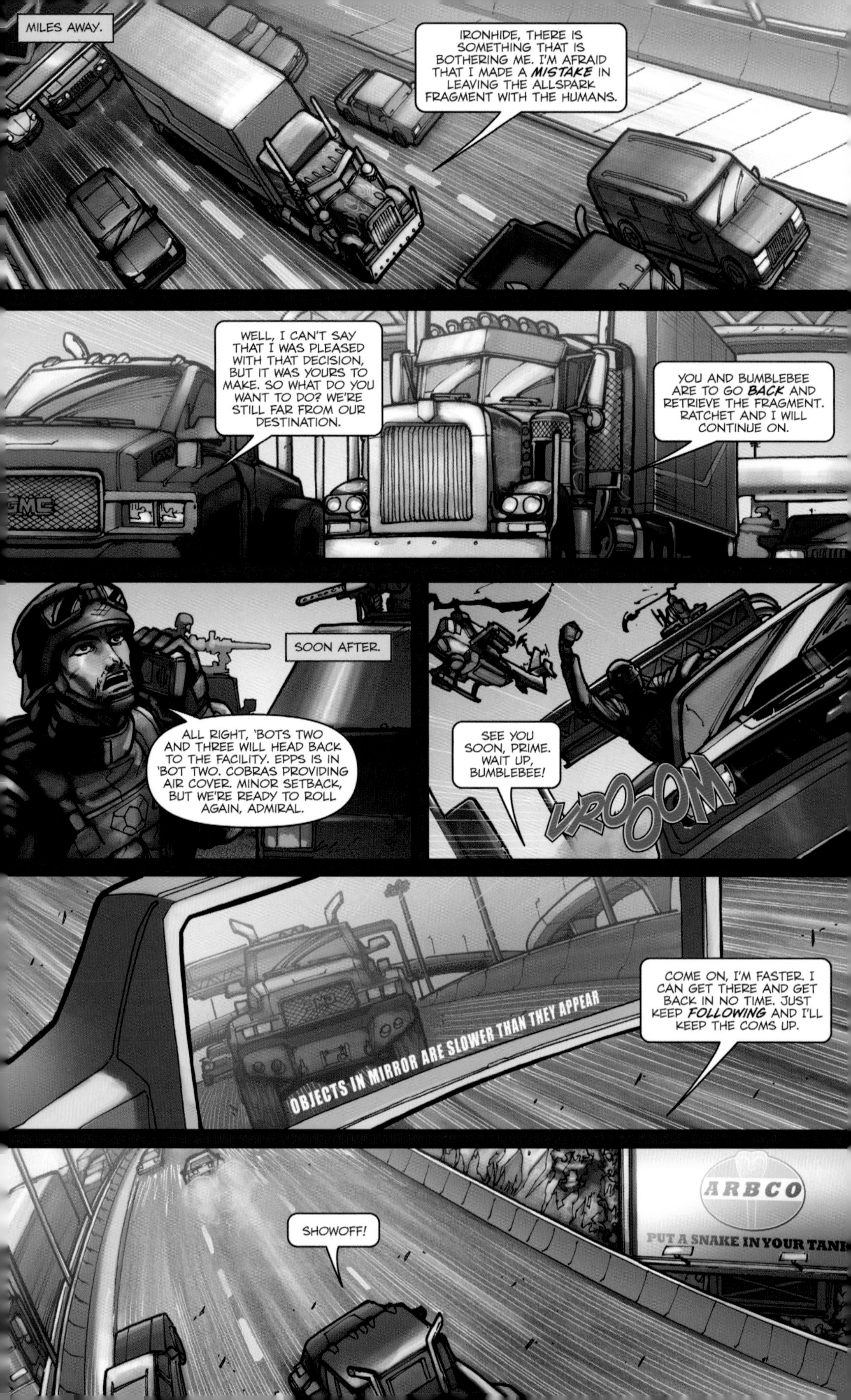
MILES AWAY.
IRONHIDE, THERE IS SOMETHING THAT IS BOTHERING ME. I'M AFRAID THAT I MADE A MISTAKE IN LEAVING THE ALLSPARK FRAGMENT WITH THE HUMANS.
WELL, I CAN'T SAY THAT I WAS PLEASED WITH THAT DECISION, BUT IT WAS YOURS TO MAKE. SO WHAT DO YOU WANT TO DO? WE'RE STILL FAR FROM OUR DESTINATION.
YOU AND BUMBLEBEE ARE TO GO BACK AND RETRIEVE THE FRAGMENT. RATCHET AND I WILL CONTINUE ON.
SOON AFTER.
ALL RIGHT, 'BOTS TWO AND THREE WILL HEAD BACK TO THE FACILITY. EPPS IS IN 'BOT TWO. COBRAS PROVIDING AIR COVER. MINOR SETBACK, BUT WE'RE READY TO ROLL AGAIN, ADMIRAL.
SEE YOU SOON, PRIME. WAIT UP, BUMBLEBEE!
VROOOM
OBJECTS IN MIRROR ARE SLOWER THAN THEY APPEAR
COME ON, I'M FASTER. I CAN GET THERE AND GET BACK IN NO TIME. JUST KEEP FOLLOWING AND I'LL KEEP THE COMS UP.
ARBCO
PUT A SNAKE IN YOUR TANK
SHOWOFF!

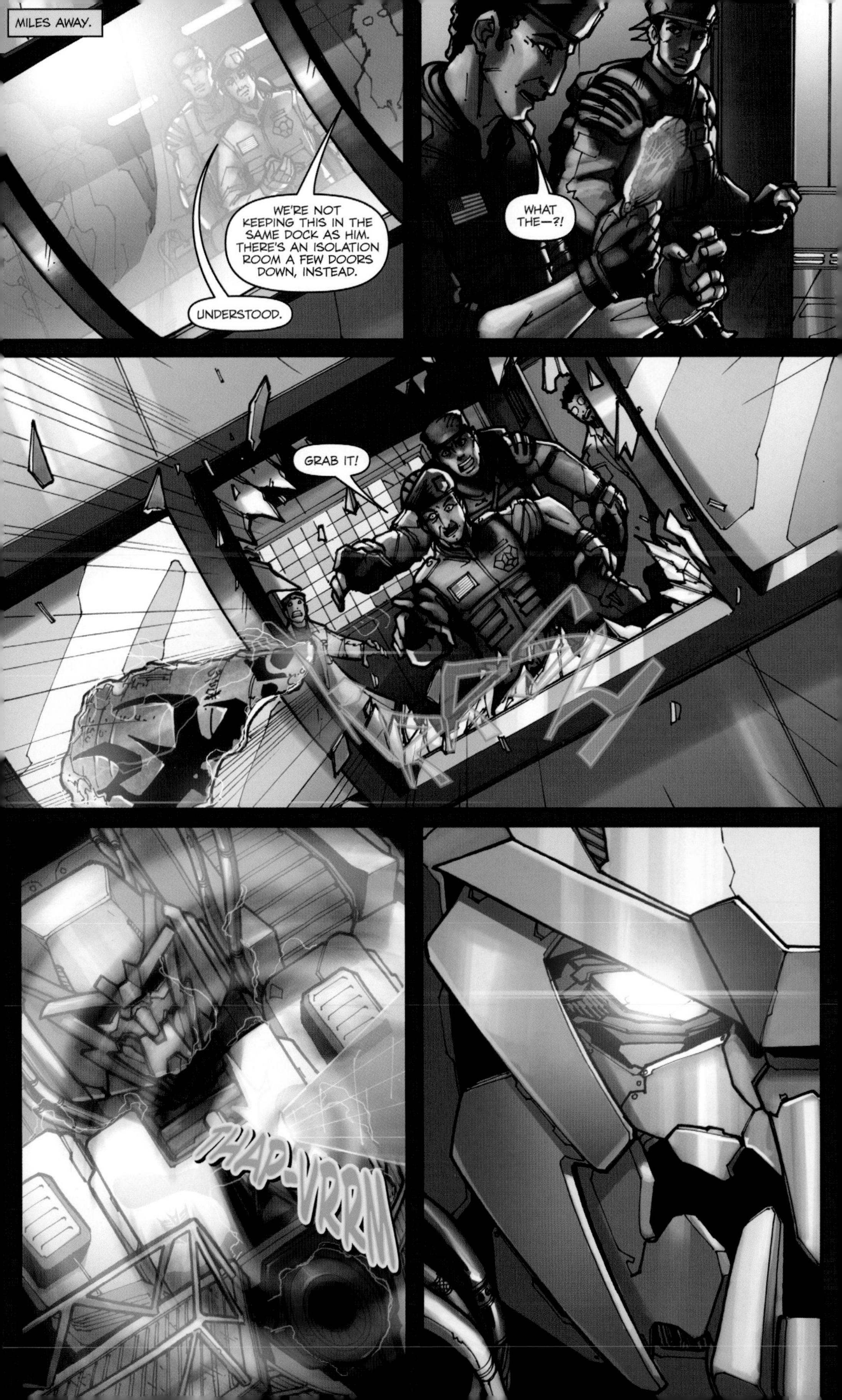
MILES AWAY.
WE'RE NOT KEEPING THIS IN THE SAME DOCK AS HIM. THERE'S AN ISOLATION ROOM A FEW DOORS DOWN, INSTEAD.
UNDERSTOOD.
WHAT THE—?!
GRAB IT!
THAP-VRRM

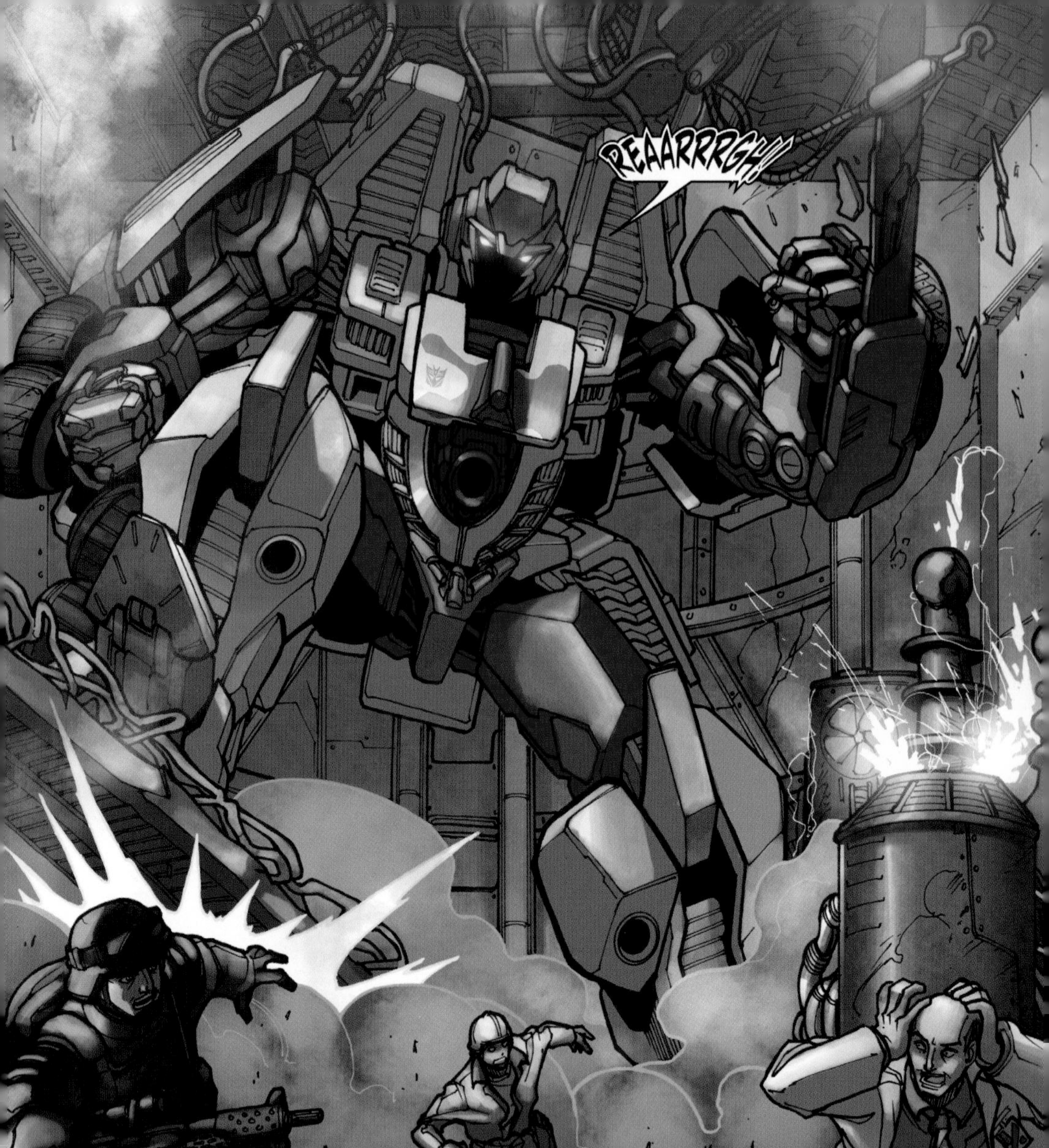
REAARRRGH!!

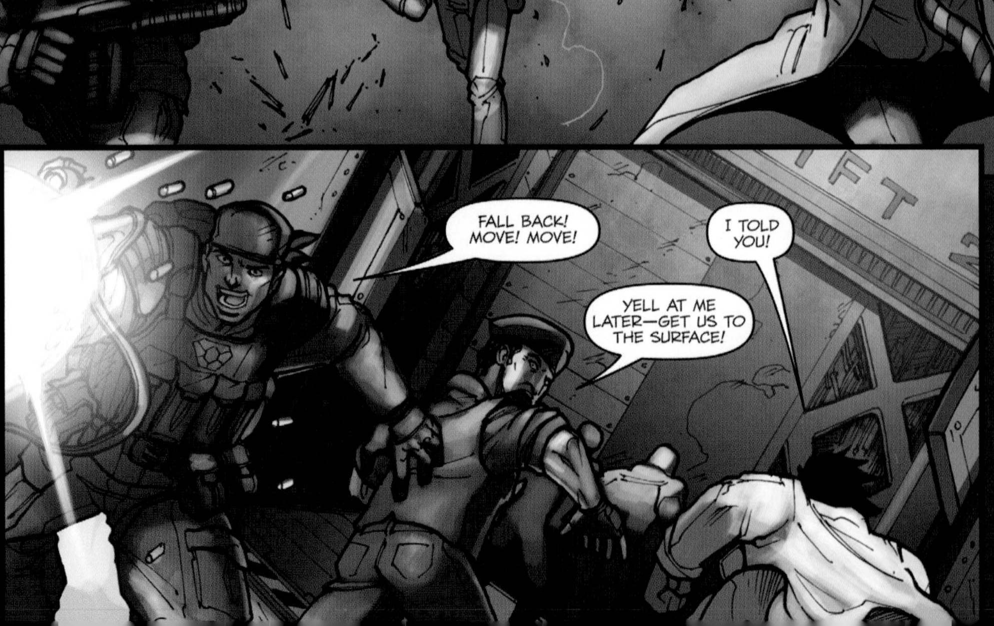
FALL BACK! MOVE! MOVE!
I TOLD YOU!
YELL AT ME LATER—GET US TO THE SURFACE!

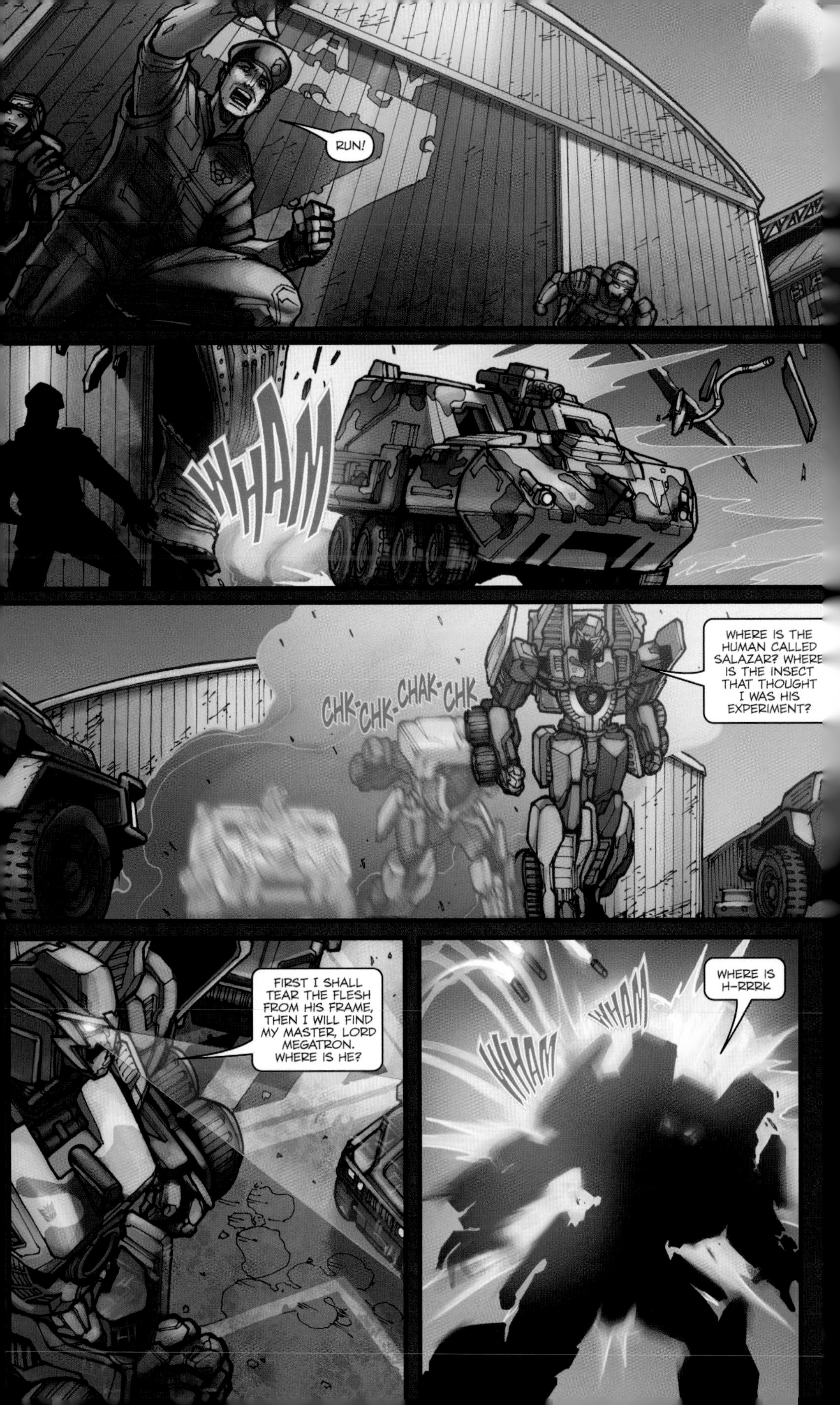
RUN!
WHAM
WHERE IS THE HUMAN CALLED SALAZAR? WHERE IS THE INSECT THAT THOUGHT I WAS HIS EXPERIMENT?
CHK-CHK-CHAK-CHK
FIRST I SHALL TEAR THE FLESH FROM HIS FRAME, THEN I WILL FIND MY MASTER, LORD MEGATRON. WHERE IS HE?
WHERE IS H-RRRK
WHAM
WHAM

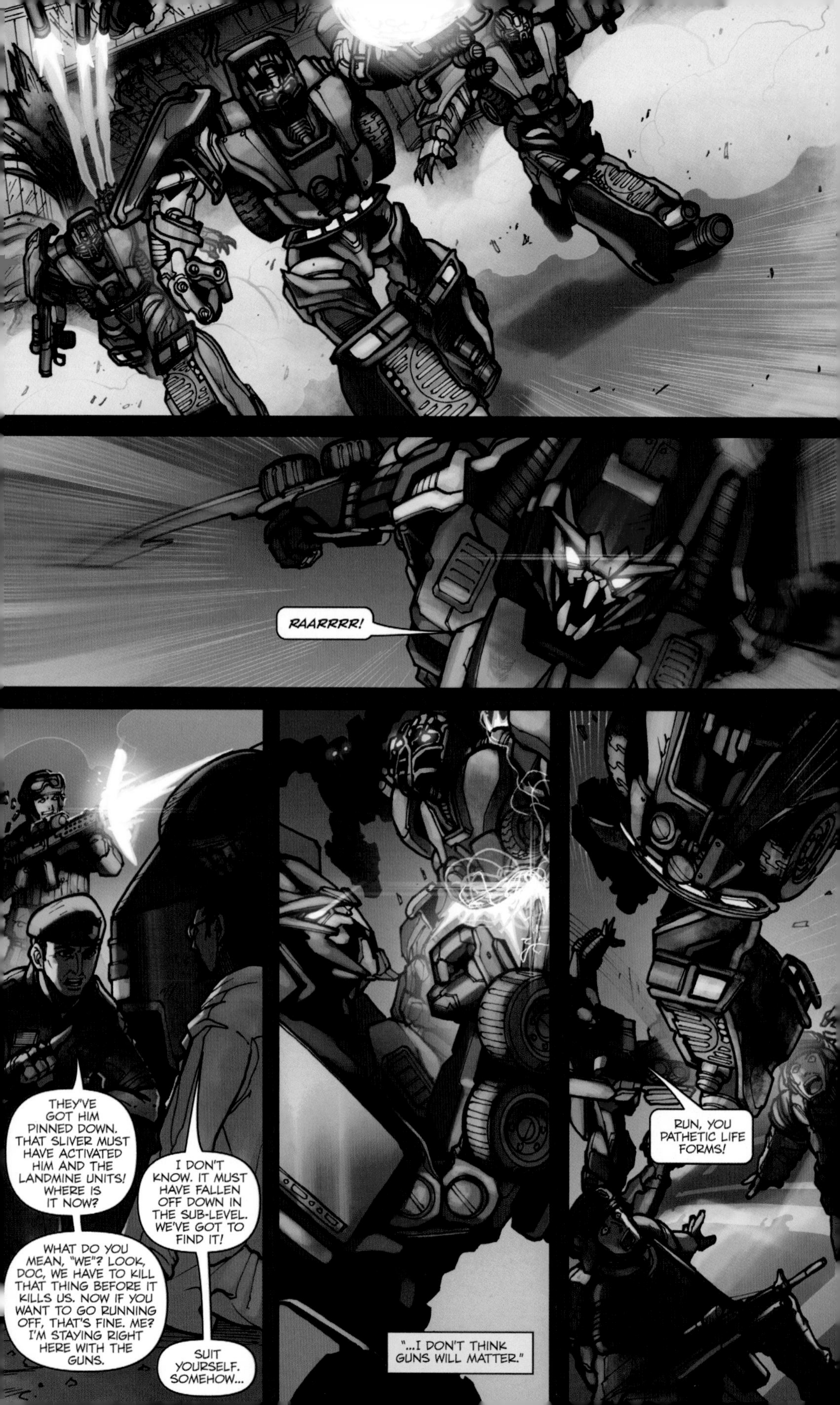
RAARRRR!
THEY'VE GOT HIM PINNED DOWN. THAT SLIVER MUST HAVE ACTIVATED HIM AND THE LANDMINE UNITS! WHERE IS IT NOW?
I DON'T KNOW. IT MUST HAVE FALLEN OFF DOWN IN THE SUB-LEVEL. WE'VE GOT TO FIND IT!
WHAT DO YOU MEAN, "WE"? LOOK, DOC, WE HAVE TO KILL THAT THING BEFORE IT KILLS US. NOW IF YOU WANT TO GO RUNNING OFF, THAT'S FINE. ME? I'M STAYING RIGHT HERE WITH THE GUNS.
SUIT YOURSELF. SOMEHOW...
"...I DON'T THINK GUNS WILL MATTER."
RUN, YOU PATHETIC LIFE FORMS!

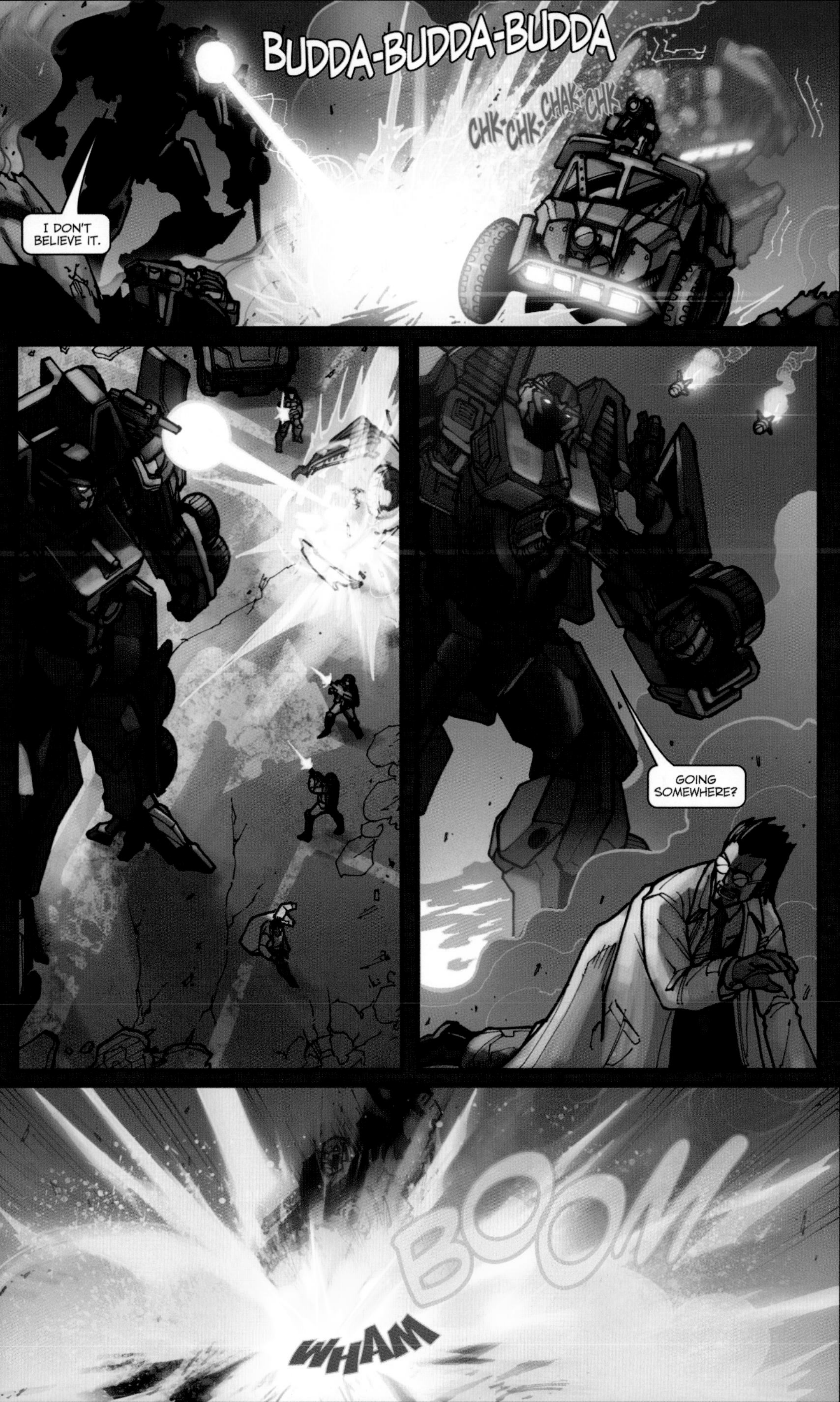
BUDDA-BUDDA-BUDDA
I DON'T BELIEVE IT.
CHK-CHK-CHAK-CHK
GOING SOMEWHERE?
BOOM
WHAM

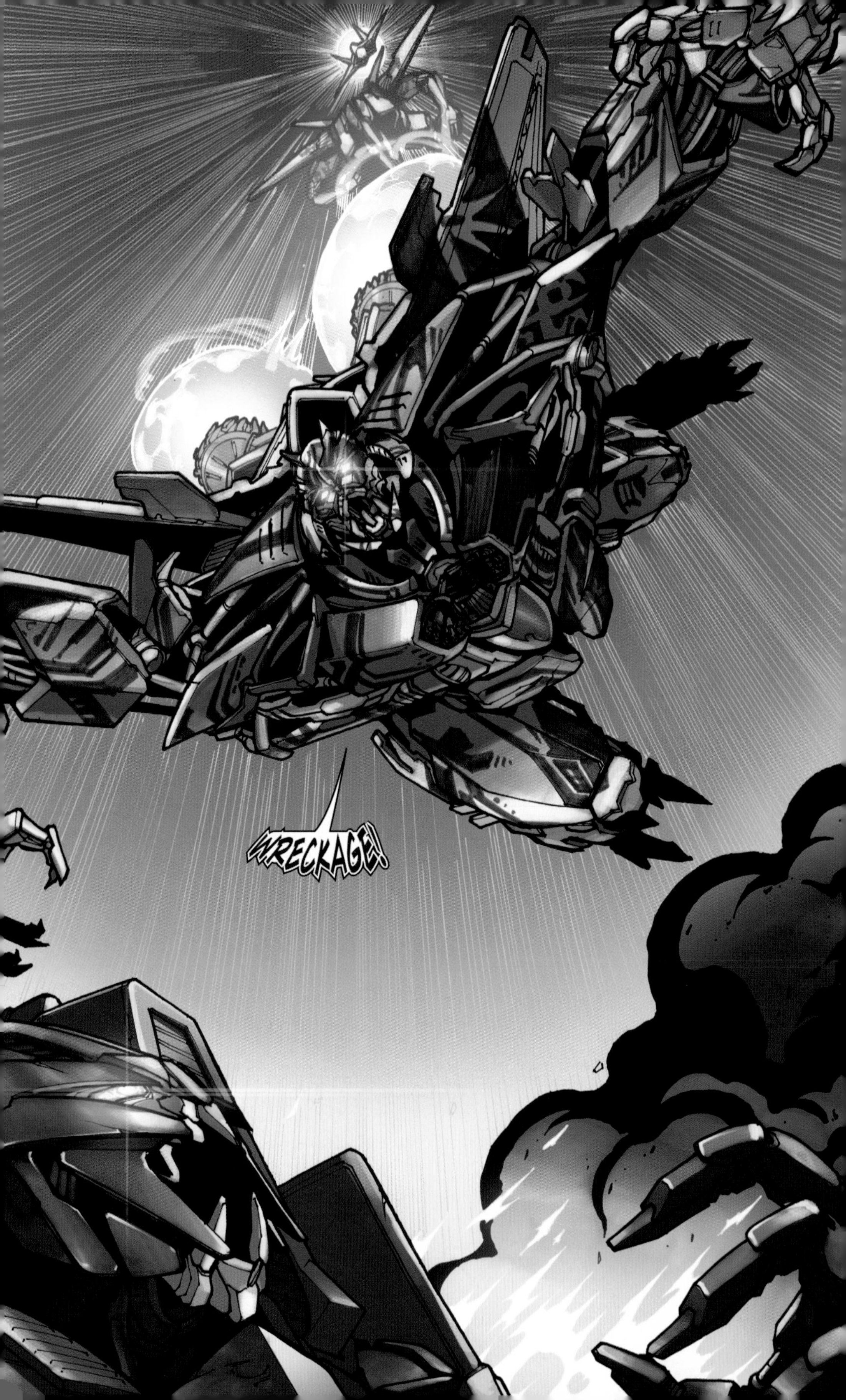
WRECKAGE!

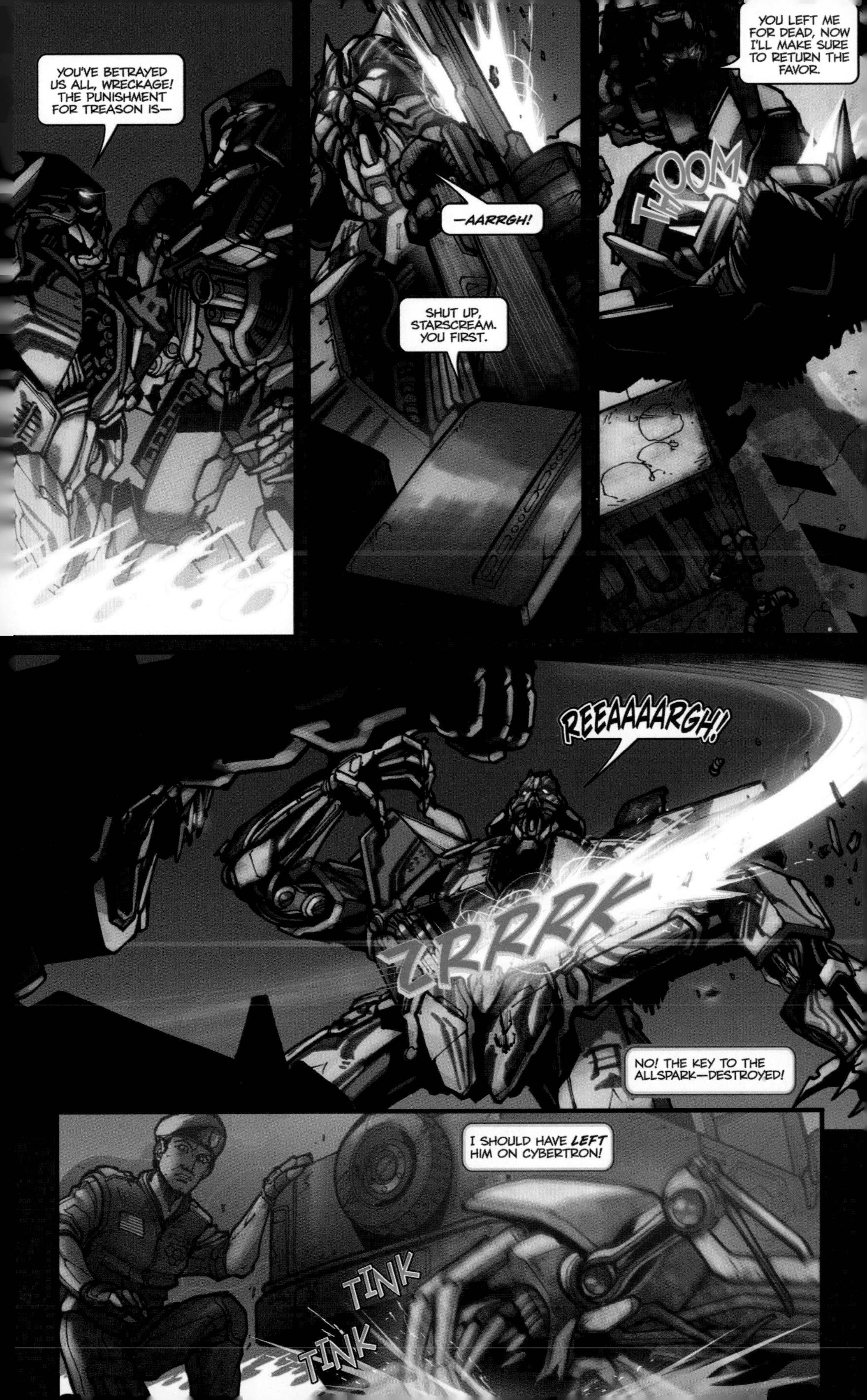

YOU'VE BETRAYED US ALL, WRECKAGE! THE PUNISHMENT FOR TREASON IS—
—AARRGH!
SHUT UP, STARSCREAM. YOU FIRST.
YOU LEFT ME FOR DEAD, NOW I'LL MAKE SURE TO RETURN THE FAVOR.
THOOM
REEAAAARGH!
ZRRRK
NO! THE KEY TO THE ALLSPARK—DESTROYED!
I SHOULD HAVE LEFT HIM ON CYBERTRON!
TINK
TINK

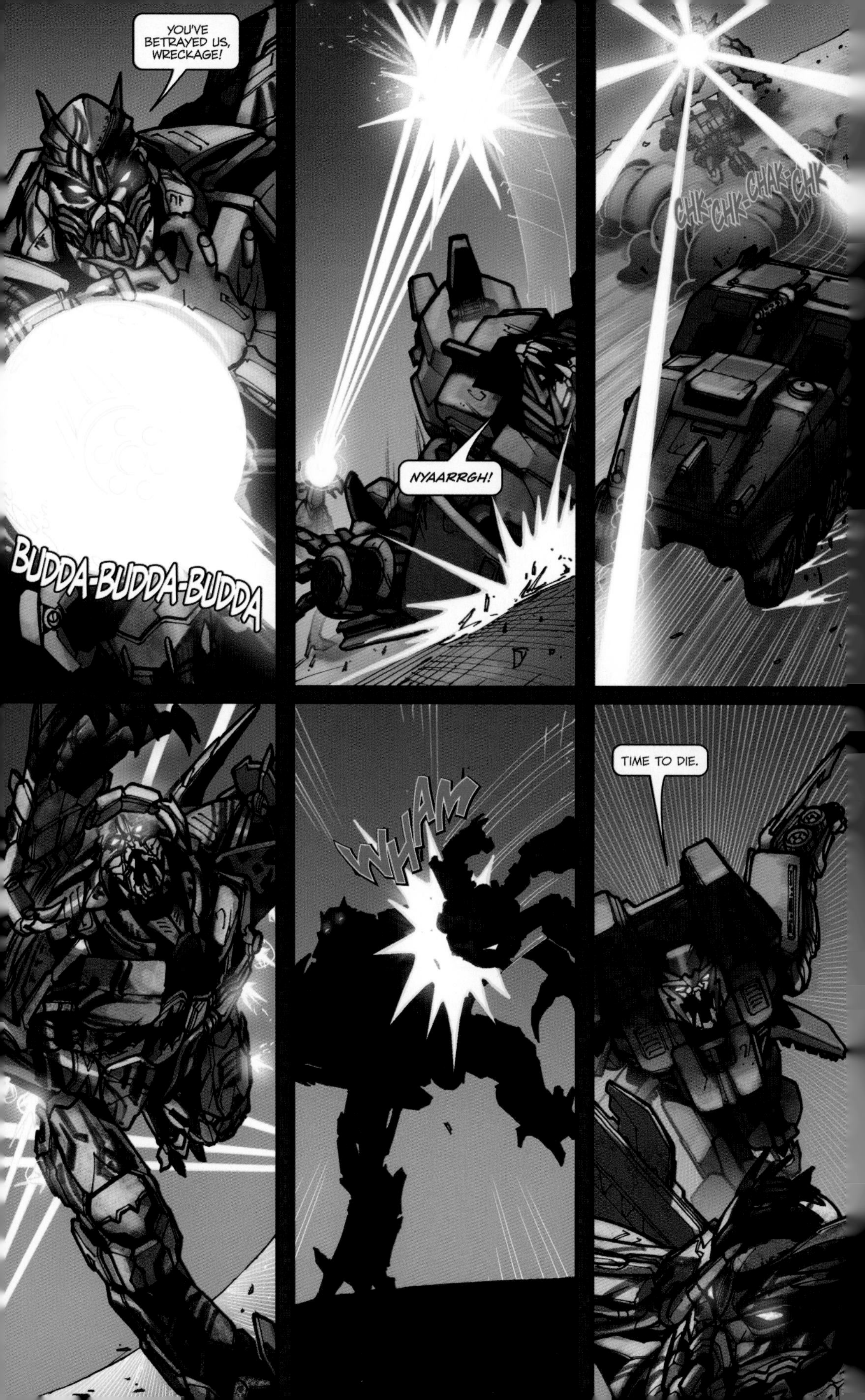
YOU'VE BETRAYED US, WRECKAGE!
BUDDA-BUDDA-BUDDA
NYAARRGH!
CHK-CHK-CHAK-CHK
WHAM
TIME TO DIE.

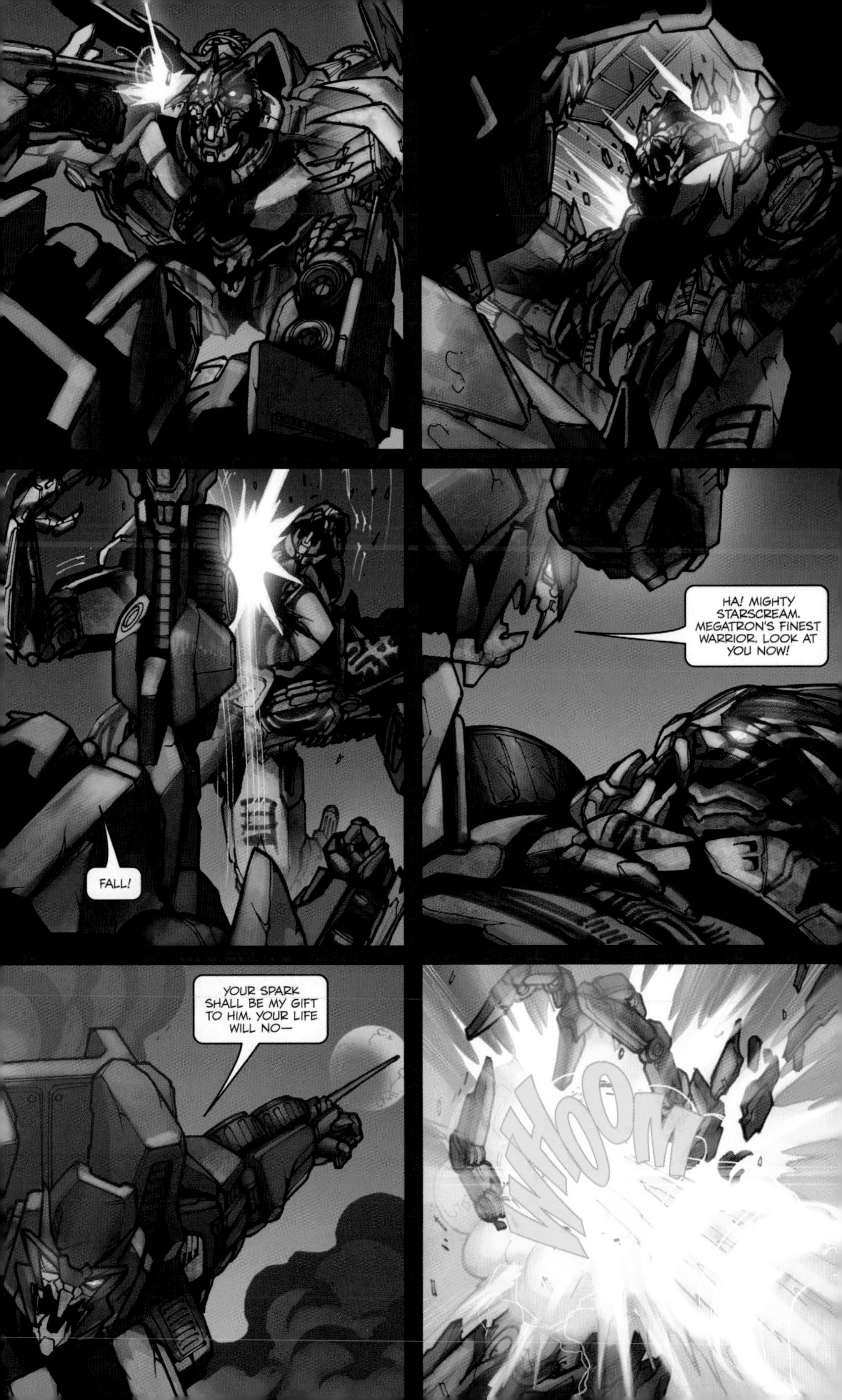
FALL!
HA! MIGHTY STARSCREAM. MEGATRON'S FINEST WARRIOR. LOOK AT YOU NOW!
YOUR SPARK SHALL BE MY GIFT TO HIM. YOUR LIFE WILL NO—
WHOOM

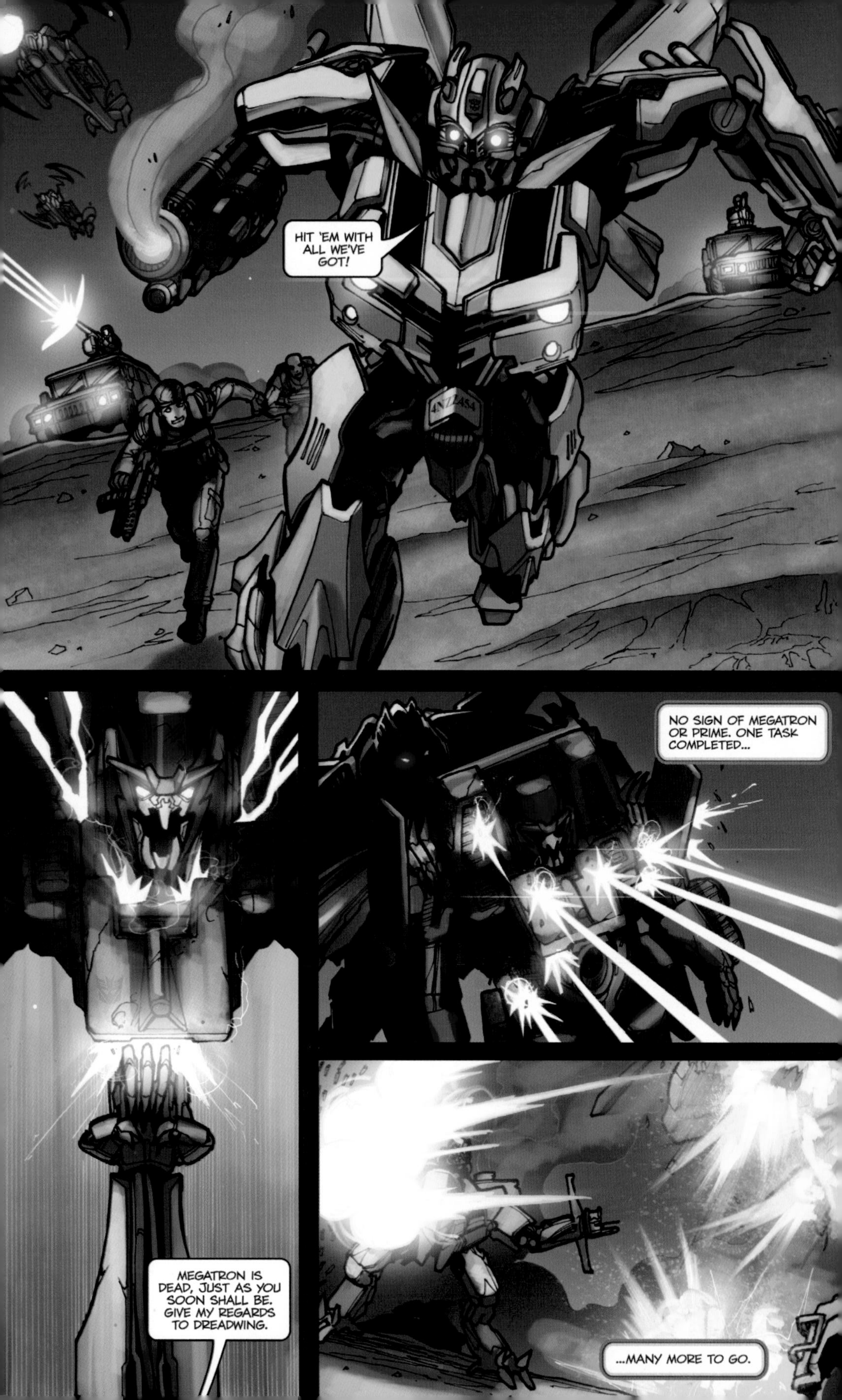
HIT 'EM WITH ALL WE'VE GOT!
NO SIGN OF MEGATRON OR PRIME. ONE TASK COMPLETED...
MEGATRON IS DEAD, JUST AS YOU SOON SHALL BE. GIVE MY REGARDS TO DREADWING.
...MANY MORE TO GO.

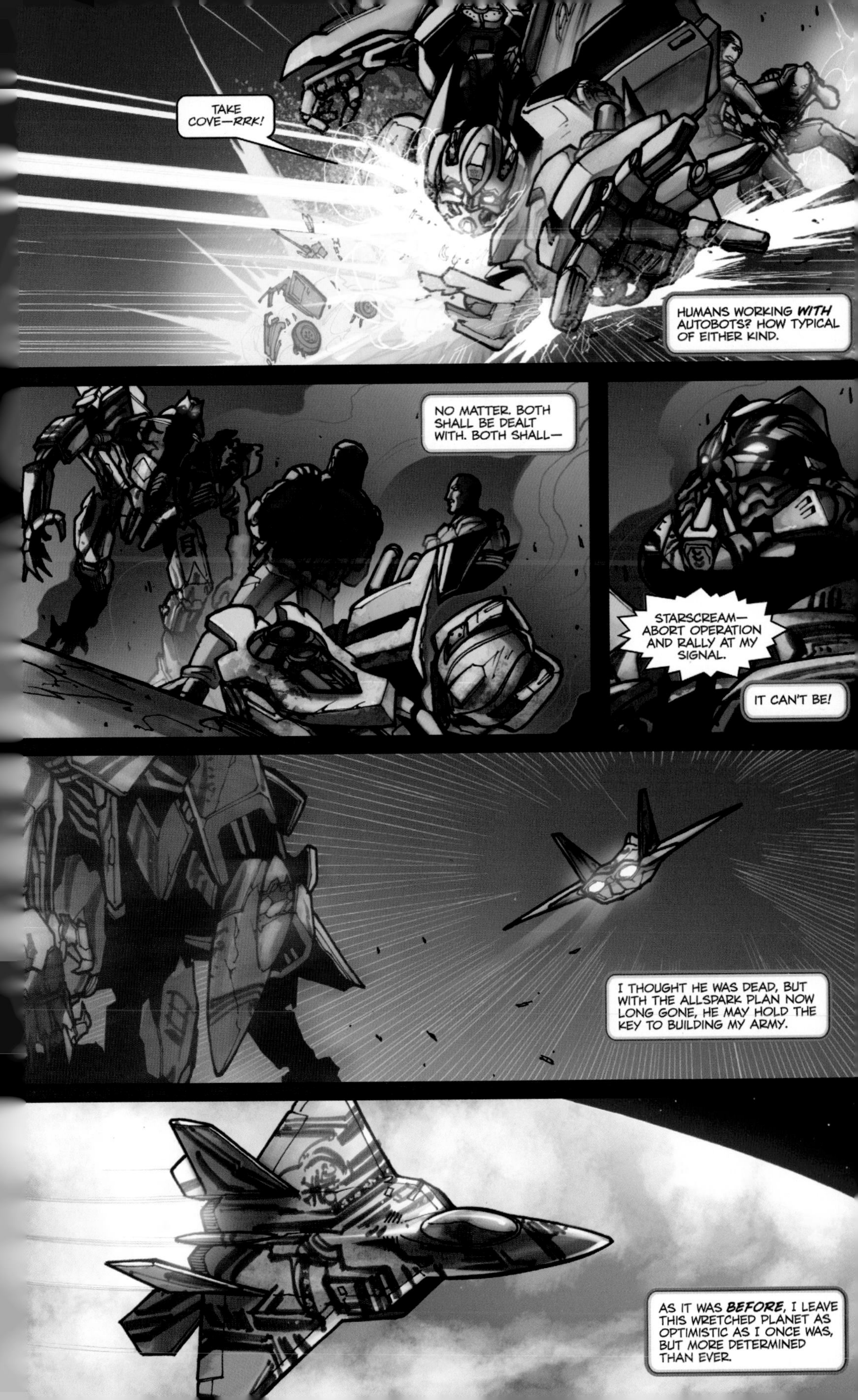
TAKE COVE—RRK!
HUMANS WORKING WITH AUTOBOTS? HOW TYPICAL OF EITHER KIND.
NO MATTER. BOTH SHALL BE DEALT WITH. BOTH SHALL—
STARSCREAM— ABORT OPERATION AND RALLY AT MY SIGNAL.
IT CAN'T BE!
I THOUGHT HE WAS DEAD, BUT WITH THE ALLSPARK PLAN NOW LONG GONE, HE MAY HOLD THE KEY TO BUILDING MY ARMY.
AS IT WAS BEFORE, I LEAVE THIS WRETCHED PLANET AS OPTIMISTIC AS I ONCE WAS, BUT MORE DETERMINED THAN EVER.

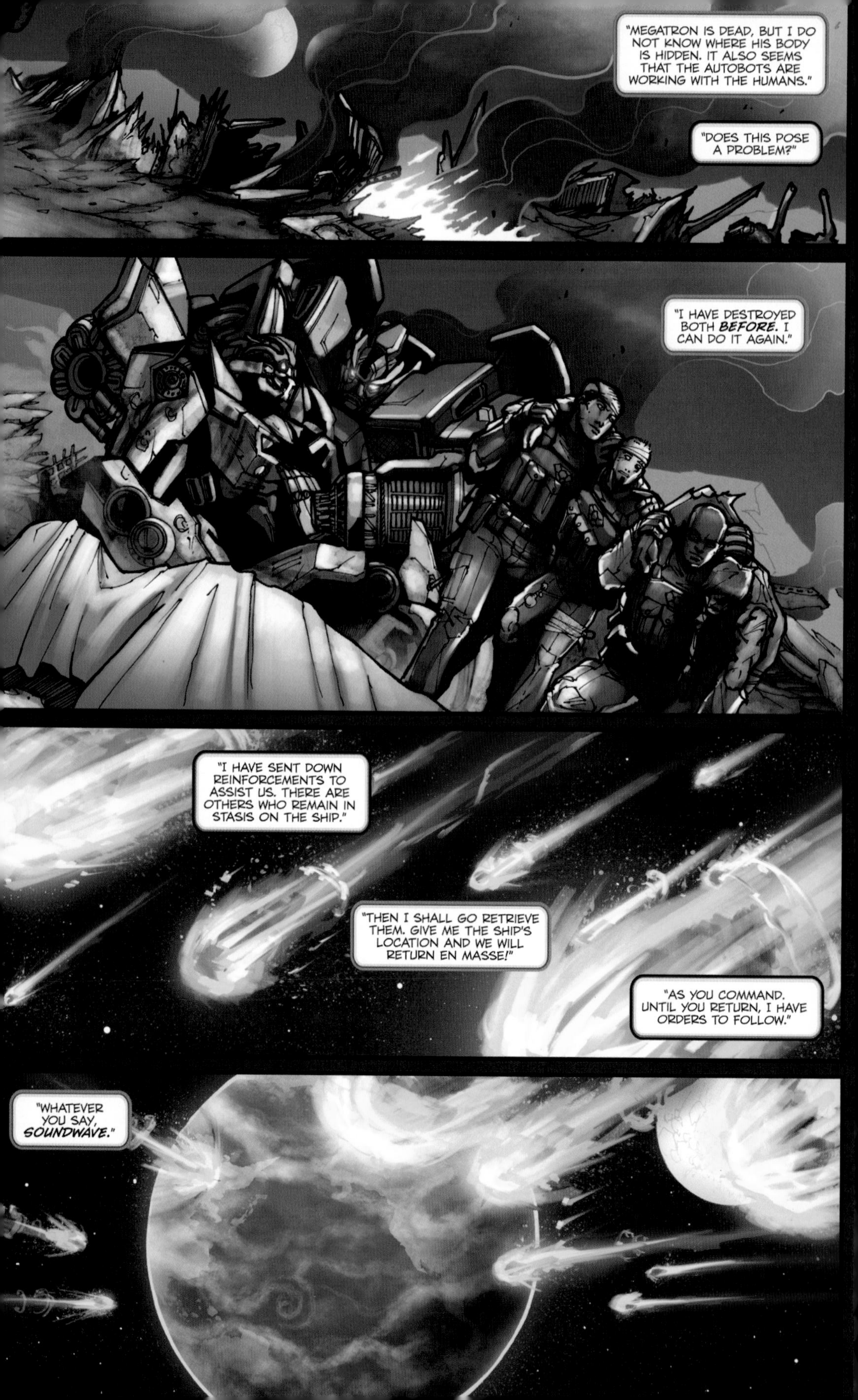
"MEGATRON IS DEAD, BUT I DO NOT KNOW WHERE HIS BODY IS HIDDEN. IT ALSO SEEMS THAT THE AUTOBOTS ARE WORKING WITH THE HUMANS."
"DOES THIS POSE A PROBLEM?"
"I HAVE DESTROYED BOTH BEFORE. I CAN DO IT AGAIN."
"I HAVE SENT DOWN REINFORCEMENTS TO ASSIST US. THERE ARE OTHERS WHO REMAIN IN STASIS ON THE SHIP."
"THEN I SHALL GO RETRIEVE THEM. GIVE ME THE SHIP'S LOCATION AND WE WILL RETURN EN MASSE!"
"AS YOU COMMAND. UNTIL YOU RETURN, I HAVE ORDERS TO FOLLOW."
"WHATEVER YOU SAY, SOUNDWAVE."